Scary Stories 3

Scary Stories 3
More Tales to Chill Your Bones
Collected from Folklore and Retold by
Alvin Schwartz

Drawings by Stephen Gammell

HarperCollins*Publishers*

Library of Congress Cataloging-in-Publication Data
Schwartz, Alvin.
  Scary Stories 3 : more tales to chill your bones / collected from folklore and retold by Alvin Schwartz ; drawings by Stephen Gammell.
      p.   cm.
  Includes bibliographical references.
  Summary: More traditional and modern-day stories of ghosts, haunts, superstitions, monsters, and horrible scary things.
  ISBN 0-06-021794-4 — ISBN 0-06-021795-2 (lib. bdg.)
  ISBN 0-06-440418-8 (pbk.)
  1. Tales.   2. Ghost stories.   3. Horror tales.   [1. Ghosts—Folklore.   2. Horror stories.   3. Folklore.]   1. Gammell, Stephen, ill.   II. Title.   II. Title: Scary stories three.
PZ8.1.S399Sb   1991   90-047474
398.2'5—dc20   CIP
                                                                       AC

Visit us on the World Wide Web!
www.harperchildrens.com

"The Wolf Girl" is based in part on "The Lobo Girl of Devil's River" by L. D. Bertillion in *Straight Texas*, Publications of the Texas Folklore Society, XIII, 1937.

"The Hog" is adapted from an untitled anecdote in *Bluenose Ghosts* by Helen Creighton. Used by permission of McGraw-Hill Ryerson Limited, Toronto. Copyright © 1957 by The Ryerson Press.

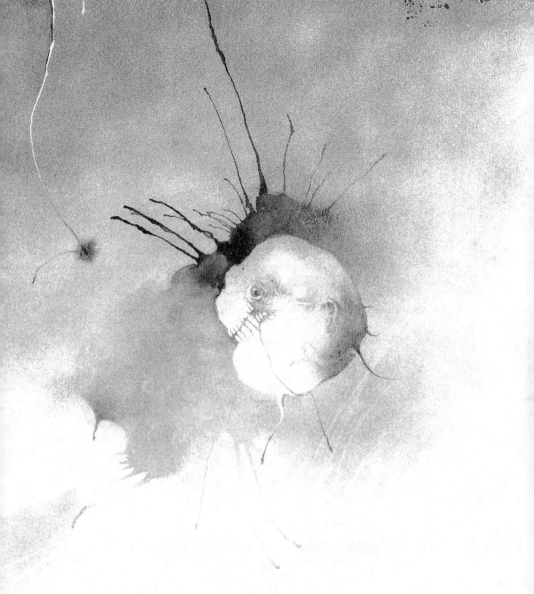

To Justin

Contents

WHOOOOOOOO?

Scary Stories 3

Boo Men

The girl was late getting home for supper. So she took a shortcut through the cemetery. But, oh, it made her nervous. When she saw another girl ahead of her, she hurried to catch up.

"Do you mind if I walk with you?" she asked. "Walking through the cemetery at night scares me."

"I know what you mean," the other girl said. "I used to feel that way myself when I was alive."

*

There are all sorts of things that scare us.

The dead scare us, for one day we will be dead like they are.

The dark scares us, for we don't know what is waiting in the dark. At night the sound of leaves rustling, or branches groaning, or someone whispering, makes us uneasy. So do footsteps coming closer. So do strange figures we think we see in the shadows—a human maybe, or a big animal, or some horrible thing we can barely make out.

People call these creatures we think we see "boo men." We imagine them, they say. But now and then a boo man turns out to be real.

Queer happenings scare us, too. We hear of a boy or a girl who was raised by an animal, a human being like us who yelps and howls and runs on all fours. The thought of it makes our flesh crawl. We hear of insects that make their nests in a person's body or of a nightmare that comes true, and we shudder. If such things really do happen, then they could happen to us.

It is from such fears that scary stories grow. This is the third book of such stories I have collected. I learned some of them from people I met. I found others, tales that had been written down, in folklore archives and in libraries. As we always do with tales we learn, I have told them in my own way.

Some stories in this book have been told only in recent times. But others have been part of our folklore for as long as we know. As one person told another, the details may have changed. But the story itself has not, for what once frightened people still frightens them.

I thought at first that one of the stories I found was a modern story. It is the one I call "The Bus Stop." I then discovered that a similar story had been told two thousand years earlier in ancient Rome. But the young woman involved was named Philinnion, not Joanna, as she is in our story.

Are the stories in this book true? The one I call "The Trouble" is true. I can't be sure about the others. Most may have at least a little truth, for strange things sometimes happen, and people love to tell about them and turn them into even better stories.

Nowadays most people say that they don't believe in ghosts and queer happenings and such. Yet they still fear the dead and the dark. And they still see boo men waiting in the shadows. And they still tell scary stories, just as people always have.

Alvin Schwartz

When Death Arrives

When Death arrives,
it usually is the end of the story.
But in these stories
it is only the beginning.

· THE APPOINTMENT ·

A sixteen-year-old boy worked on his grandfather's horse farm. One morning he drove a pickup truck into town on an errand. While he was walking along the main street, he saw Death. Death beckoned to him.

The boy drove back to the farm as fast as he could and told his grandfather what had happened. "Give me the truck," he begged. "I'll go to the city. He'll never find me there."

His grandfather gave him the truck, and the boy sped away. After he left, his grandfather went into town looking for Death. When he found him, he asked, "Why did you frighten my grandson that way? He is only sixteen. He is too young to die."

"I am sorry about that," said Death. "I did not mean to beckon to him. But I *was* surprised to see him here. You see, I have an appointment with him this afternoon—in the city."

· *THE BUS STOP* ·

Ed Cox was driving home from work in a rainstorm. While he waited for a traffic light to change, he saw a young woman standing alone at a bus stop. She had no umbrella and was soaking wet.

"Are you going toward Farmington?" he called.

"Yes, I am," she said.

"Would you like a ride home?"

"I would," she said, and she got in. "My name is Joanna Finney. Thank you for rescuing me."

"I'm Ed Cox," he said, "and you're welcome."

On the way they talked and talked. She told him about her family and her job and where she had gone to school, and he told her about himself. By the time they got to her house, the rain had stopped.

"I'm glad it rained," Ed said. "Would you like to go out tomorrow after work?"

"I'd love to," Joanna said.

She asked him to meet her at the bus stop, since it was near her office. They had such a good time, they went out many times after that. Always they would meet at the bus stop, and off they would go. Ed liked her more each time he saw her.

But one night when they had a date to go out, Joanna did not appear. Ed waited at the bus stop for almost an hour. "Maybe something is wrong," he thought, and he drove to her house in Farmington.

An older woman came to the door. "I'm Ed Cox," he said. "Maybe Joanna told you about me. I had a date with her tonight. We were supposed to meet at the bus stop near her office. But she didn't show up. Is she all right?"

The woman looked at him as if he had said something strange. "I am Joanna's mother," she said slowly. "Joanna isn't here now. But why don't you come in?"

Ed pointed to a picture on the mantel. "That looks just like her," he said.

"It did, once," her mother replied. "But that picture was taken when she was your age—about twenty years ago. A few days later she was waiting in the rain at that bus stop. A car hit her, and she was killed."

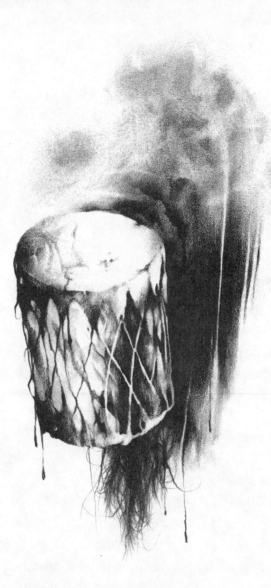

· *FASTER AND FASTER* ·

Sam and his cousin Bob went walking in the woods. The only sounds were leaves rustling and, now and again, a bird chirping. "It's so quiet here," Bob whispered.

But that soon changed. After a few minutes the two boys

started whooping and hollering and chasing one another around. Sam ducked behind a tree. When Bob came by, Sam jumped out at him. Then Bob raced ahead and hid behind a bush. When he looked down, there at his feet was an old drum.

"Sam! See what I found," he called. "It looks like a tom-tom. I bet it's a hundred years old."

"Look at the red stains on it," said Sam. "I bet it's somebody's blood. Let's get out of here."

But Bob could not resist trying the drum. He sat on the ground and held it between his legs. He beat on it with one hand, then the other, slowly at first, then faster and faster, almost as if he could not stop.

Suddenly there were shouts in the woods and the sound of hoofbeats. A cloud of dust rose from behind a line of trees. Then men on horseback galloped toward them.

"Bob! Let's go!" Sam shouted. He began to run. "Hurry!"

Bob dropped the drum and ran after him.

Sam heard the twang of a bow firing an arrow. Then he heard Bob scream. When Sam turned, he saw Bob pitch forward, dead. But there was no arrow in his body, and there was no wound. And when the police searched, there were no men on horseback, and there were no hoof-prints—and there was no drum.

The only sounds were leaves rustling and, now and again, a bird chirping.

· *JUST DELICIOUS* ·

George Flint loved to eat. Each day at noon he closed his camera shop for two hours and went home for a big lunch his wife Mina cooked for him. George was a bully, and Mina was a timid woman who did everything he asked because she was afraid of him.

On his way home for lunch one day, George stopped at the butcher shop and bought a pound of liver. He loved liver. He would have Mina cook it for dinner that night. Despite all his complaints about her, she was a very good cook.

While George ate his lunch, Mina told him that a rich old woman in town had died. Her body was in the church next door. It was in an open coffin. Anyone who wanted to see her could. As usual, George was not interested in what Mina had to say. "I've got to go back to work," he told her.

After he left, Mina began to cook the liver. She added vegetables and spices and simmered it all afternoon, just the way George liked it. When she thought it was done, she cut off a small piece and tasted it. It was delicious, the best she had ever made. She ate a second piece. Then a third. It was so good, she could not stop eating it.

It was only when the liver was all gone that she thought of George. He would be coming home soon. What would he do when he found that she had eaten all of the liver? Some men would laugh—but not George. He would be angry and mean, and she did not want to face that again. But where could she get another piece of liver that late in the day?

Then she remembered the old woman lying in the church next door waiting to be buried. . . .

George said he never had a better dinner. "Have some liver, Mina," he said. "It's just delicious."

"I'm not hungry," she said. "You finish it."

That night, after George had fallen asleep, Mina sat in bed trying to read. But all she could think about was what she had done. Then she thought she heard a woman's voice.

"Who has my liver?" it asked. "Who has it?"

Was it her imagination? Was she dreaming?

Now the voice was closer. "Who has my liver?" it asked. "Who has it?"

Mina wanted to run. "No, no," she whispered. "I don't have it. I don't have your liver."

Now the voice was right next to her. "Who has my liver?" it asked. "Who has it?"

Mina froze with terror. She pointed to George. "He does," she said. "*He* has it!"

Suddenly the light went out—and George screamed, and screamed.

· *HELLO, KATE!* ·

Tom Connors was on his way to a dance in the next village. It was a long walk through fields and woods. But it was a soft, sweet evening and he loved dancing, so Tom didn't mind.

He had gone only a short distance when he noticed a young woman following him. "Maybe she is going to the dance," he thought, and he stopped and waited for her. As the woman got closer, he saw that it was Kate Faherty. They had danced together many times.

He was about to call "Hello, Kate!" when suddenly he remembered that Kate was dead. She had died last year, yet there she was all dressed up for the dance. Tom wanted to run, but somehow it didn't seem right to run from Kate. He turned and started to walk away as fast as he could, but Kate followed him. He took a shortcut across a field, but still she followed.

When he got to the dance hall, she was right behind him. There were a lot of people standing outside, and Tom tried to lose Kate in the crowd. He worked his way to the side of the building, then squeezed up against the wall behind some people.

But Kate followed. She came so close she brushed up against him. Then she stopped and waited. He wanted to say "Hello, Kate!" just the way he did when she was alive. But he was so frightened he couldn't speak. Her eyes looked into his eyes—and she vanished.

· THE BLACK DOG ·

It was eleven o'clock at night. Peter Rothberg was in bed on the second floor of the old house where he lived alone. It had gotten so chilly, he went downstairs to turn up the heat.

As Peter was on his way back to bed, a black dog ran down the stairs. It passed him and disappeared into the darkness. "Where did *you* come from?" Peter said. He had never seen the dog before.

He turned on all the lights and looked in every room. He could not find the dog anywhere. He went outside and brought in the two watchdogs he kept in the backyard. But they acted as if they were the only dogs in the house.

The next night, again at eleven o'clock, Peter was in his bedroom. He heard what sounded like a dog walking around in the room above him. He dashed upstairs and threw open the door. The room was empty. He looked under the bed. He looked in the closet. Nothing. But when he got back to his bedroom, he heard a dog running down the stairs. It was the black dog. He tried to follow it, but again he could not find where it had gone.

From then on, every night at eleven, Peter heard the dog walking in the room above him. The room was always empty. But after he left, the dog would come out of hiding, run down the stairs, and disappear.

One night Peter's neighbor waited with him for the dog. At the usual time they heard it above them. Then they heard it on the stairs. When they went out into the hall, it was standing at the foot of the stairs looking up at them.

The neighbor whistled, and the dog wagged its tail. Then it was gone.

Things went on this way until the night Peter decided to bring his watchdogs into the house again. Maybe this time they would find the black dog and drive it away. Just before eleven he took them up to his bedroom and left the door open.

Then he heard the black dog moving around above him. His dogs pricked up their ears and ran to the door. Suddenly they bared their teeth and snarled and backed away. Peter could not see the black dog or hear it, but he was sure that it had entered his room. His dogs barked and snapped. They darted forward nervously, then backed away again.

Suddenly one of them yelped. It began bleeding, then dropped to the floor, its neck torn open. A minute later it was dead. Peter's other dog backed into a corner, whimpering. Then everything was still.

The next night Peter's neighbor came back with a pistol. Again they waited in his bedroom. At eleven o'clock the black dog came down the stairs. As before, it looked up at them and wagged its tail. When they started toward it with the pistol, it growled and disappeared.

That was the last Peter saw of the black dog. But it did not mean that the dog was gone. Now and then, always at eleven, he heard it moving around above him. Once he heard it running down the stairs. He never managed to see it again. But he knew that it was there.

· *FOOTSTEPS* ·

Liz was doing her homework at the dining-room table. Her younger sister Sarah was asleep upstairs. Their mother was out, but she was expected back any minute.

When the front door opened and shut, Liz called, "Hello, Mama!" But her mother didn't answer. And the footsteps Liz heard were heavier, like a man's.

"Who's there?" she called. No one replied. She heard whoever it was walk through the living room, then up the stairs to the second floor. The footsteps moved from one bedroom to another.

Again Liz called, "Who's there?" The footsteps stopped. Then she thought, "Oh, my God! Sarah is in her bedroom." She ran upstairs to Sarah's room. Only Sarah was there, and she was asleep. Liz looked in the other rooms, but found no one. She went back down to the dining room, scared out of her wits.

Soon she heard footsteps again. They were coming down the stairs, into the living room. Now they went into the kitchen. Then the door between the kitchen and the dining room slowly began to open. . . .

"Get out!" Liz screamed. The door slowly closed. The footsteps moved out of the kitchen, through the living room, toward the front door. The door opened and shut.

Liz ran to the window to see who it was. No one was in sight. Nor were there any footprints in the fresh snow that had been falling.

· LIKE CATS' EYES ·

As Jim Brand lay dying, his wife left him with his nurse and went into the next room to rest. She sat in the dark staring into the night. Suddenly Mrs. Brand saw headlights come rapidly up the driveway.

"Oh, no," she thought. "I don't want visitors now, not now." But it wasn't a car bringing a visitor. It was an old hearse with maybe a half dozen small men hanging from the sides. At least, that's what it looked like.

The hearse screeched to a stop. The men jumped off and stared up at her, their eyes glowing with a soft, yellow light, like cats' eyes. She watched with horror as they disappeared into the house.

An instant later they were back, lifting something into the hearse. Then they drove off at high speed, wheels squealing, the gravel in the driveway flying in all directions.

At that moment the nurse came in to say that Jim Brand had died.

On the Edge

*You will say
that these stories
could not happen.
Yet some say
they did happen.*

· *BESS* ·

John Nicholas raised horses. He had many horses of all kinds, but his favorite was Bess, a gentle old mare he had grown up with. He no longer rode her, for all she could do now was just amble along. Bess spent her days grazing peacefully in a meadow.

That summer, for the fun of it, John Nicholas went into a fortune-teller's booth. The fortune-teller studied her cards. "I see danger ahead for you," she said. "Your favorite horse will cause you to die. I don't know when, but it will happen. It is in the cards."

John Nicholas laughed. The idea that Bess would cause his death was nonsense. She was as dangerous as a bowl of soup. Yet from then on, whenever he saw her, he remembered the fortune-teller's warning.

That fall a farmer from the other end of the county asked if he could have Bess. He had been thinking that the old horse would be perfect for his children to ride.

"That's a good idea," John said. "It would be fun for them, and it would give Bess something to do."

Later John told his wife about it. "Now Bess won't kill me," he said, and they both laughed.

A few months later, he saw the farmer who had taken her. "How's my Bess?" he asked.

"Oh, she was fine for a while," the farmer said. "The children loved her. Then she got sick. I had to shoot her to put her out of her misery. It was a shame."

Despite himself, John breathed a sigh of relief. He had often wondered if in some crazy way, through some

strange accident, Bess would kill him. Now, of course, she could not.

"I'd like to see her," said John. "Just to say good-bye. She was my favorite."

The bones of the dead horse were in a far corner of the man's farm. John kneeled down and patted Bess's sun-bleached skull. Just then a rattlesnake, which had made its home inside the skull, sank its fangs into John Nicholas's arm and killed him.

· HAROLD ·

When it got hot in the valley, Thomas and Alfred drove their cows up to a cool, green pasture in the mountains to graze. Usually they stayed there with the cows for two months. Then they brought them down to the valley again.

The work was easy enough, but, oh, it was boring. All day the two men tended their cows. At night they went

back to the tiny hut where they lived. They ate supper and worked in the garden and went to sleep. It was always the same.

Then Thomas had an idea that changed everything. "Let's make a doll the size of a man," he said. "It would be fun to make, and we could put it in the garden to scare away the birds."

"It should look like Harold," Alfred said. Harold was a farmer they both hated. They made the doll out of old sacks stuffed with straw. They gave it a pointy nose like Harold's and tiny eyes like his. Then they added dark hair and a twisted frown. Of course they also gave it Harold's name.

Each morning on their way to the pasture, they tied

Harold to a pole in the garden to scare away the birds. Each night they brought him inside so that he wouldn't get ruined if it rained.

When they were feeling playful, they would talk to him. One of them might say, "How are the vegetables growing today, Harold?" Then the other, making believe he was Harold, would answer in a crazy voice, "*Very* slowly." They both would laugh, but not Harold.

Whenever something went wrong, they took it out on Harold. They would curse at him, even kick him or punch him. Sometimes one of them would take the food they were eating (which they both were sick of) and smear it on the doll's face. "How do you like that stew, Harold?" he would ask. "Well, you'd better eat it—or else." Then the two men would howl with laughter.

One night, after Thomas had wiped Harold's face with food, Harold grunted.

"Did you hear that?" Alfred asked.

"It was Harold," Thomas said. "I was watching him when it happened. I can't believe it."

"How could he grunt?" Alfred asked. "He's just a sack of straw. It's not possible."

"Let's throw him in the fire," said Thomas, "and that will be that."

"Let's not do anything stupid," said Alfred. "We don't know what's going on. When we move the cows down, we'll leave him behind. For now, let's just keep an eye on him."

So they left Harold sitting in a corner of the hut. They didn't talk to him or take him outside anymore. Now and then the doll grunted, but that was all. After a few days they decided there was nothing to be afraid of. Maybe a mouse or some insects had gotten inside Harold and were making those sounds.

So Thomas and Alfred went back to their old ways. Each morning they put Harold out in the garden, and each night they brought him back into the hut. When they felt playful, they joked with him. When they felt mean, they treated him as badly as ever.

Then one night Alfred noticed something that frightened him. "Harold is growing," he said.

"I was thinking the same thing," Thomas said.

"Maybe it's just our imagination," Alfred replied. "We have been up here on this mountain too long."

The next morning, while they were eating, Harold stood up and walked out of the hut. He climbed up on the roof and trotted back and forth, like a horse on its hind legs. All day and all night long he trotted like that.

In the morning Harold climbed down and stood in a far corner of the pasture. The men had no idea what he would do next. They were afraid.

They decided to take the cows down into the valley that same day. When they left, Harold was nowhere in sight. They felt as if they had escaped a great danger and began joking and singing. But when they had gone only a mile or two, they realized they had forgotten to bring the milking stools.

Neither one wanted to go back for them, but the stools would cost a lot to replace. "There really is nothing to be afraid of," they told one another. "After all, what could a doll do?"

They drew straws to see which one would go back. It was Thomas. "I'll catch up with you," he said, and Alfred walked on toward the valley.

When Alfred came to a rise in the path, he looked back for Thomas. He did not see him anywhere. But he did see Harold. The doll was on the roof of the hut again. As Alfred watched, Harold kneeled and stretched out a bloody skin to dry in the sun.

· *THE DEAD HAND* ·

The village huddled on the edge of a vast swamp. As far as one could see, there were soggy meadows, holes filled with black water, and glistening sheets of wet, spongy peat. Skeletons of giant trees—"snags," the people called them— rose up out of the muck, their dead branches reaching out like long, twisted arms.

During the day, the men in the village cut the peat and hauled it home to dry and sell for fuel. But when the sun went down, and the wind, sighing and moaning, came in from the sea, the men were quick to leave. Strange creatures took over the swamp at night, and some even came into the village—that's what everyone said. People were so afraid, they would not go out alone after dark.

Young Tom Pattison was the only person in the village who did not believe in these creatures. On his way home from work, he'd whisper to his friends, "There's one!" and they would jump and run. And Tom would laugh and laugh.

Finally some of his friends turned on him. "If you know so much," they said, "go back into the swamp some night and see what comes of it."

"I'll do it," said Tom. "I work out there every day. Not once have I ever seen anything to frighten me. Why should it be different at night? Tomorrow night I'll take my lantern and walk out to the willow snag. If I get scared and run, I'll never make fun of you again."

The next night the men went to Tom Pattison's house to see him on his way. Thick clouds covered the moon. It was the blackest of nights. When they arrived, Tom's mother was pleading with him not to go.

"I'll be all right," he said. "There's nothing to be afraid of. Don't be foolish like the rest."

He took his lantern and, singing to himself, headed down the spongy path toward the willow snag.

Some of the young men wondered if Tom wasn't right. Maybe they were afraid of things that did not exist. A few decided to follow him and see for themselves, but they stayed far behind in case he ran into trouble. They were sure they saw dark shapes moving about. But Tom's lantern kept bobbing up and down, and Tom's songs kept floating back to them, and nothing happened.

Finally they caught sight of the willow snag. There was Tom standing in a circle of light, looking this way and that. All of a sudden the wind blew out his lantern, and Tom stopped singing. The men stood stock-still in the blackness, waiting for something awful to happen.

The clouds shifted and the moon came out. There was Tom again. Only now he had his back pushed up against the willow snag, and he had his arms out in front of him, as if he were fighting something off. From where the men stood, it looked like dark shapes were swirling in around him. Then the clouds covered the moon again. Once more it was as black as pitch.

When the moon came out again, Tom was hanging on to the willow snag with one arm. His other arm was stretched out in front of him, as if something was pulling it. It looked to the men as if a rotting, moldy hand with no arm—a dead hand—had grabbed Tom's hand. With one

final wrench, whatever had hold of Tom jerked him into the muck. That's what the men said.

When the clouds blotted out the moon once more, the men turned and ran through the blackness toward the village. Again and again they lost the path and fell into the muck and water holes. In the end they crawled back on their hands and knees. But Tom Pattison was not with them.

In the morning the people searched everywhere for Tom. Finally they gave him up for lost.

A few weeks later, toward evening, the villagers heard a cry. It was Tom's mother. She was rushing down the path from the swamp, shouting and waving. When she was sure the villagers had spotted her, she turned and ran back. Off they went after her.

They found young Tom Pattison by the willow snag, groaning and gibbering as if he had lost his mind. He kept pointing with one hand at something only he could see. Where his other hand should have been, there was nothing but a ragged stump oozing blood. The hand had been ripped clean off.

Everybody said it was the dead hand that had done it. But nobody really knows. Nobody will ever know—except Tom Pattison. And he never spoke another word again.

· SUCH THINGS HAPPEN ·

When Bill Nelson's cow stopped giving milk, he called the veterinarian. "There's nothing wrong with that cow," the vet said. "She's just stubborn. That, or some witch got hold of her." Bill and the vet both laughed.

"That old hag, Addie Fitch, I guess she's the closest we've got to a witch around here," the vet said. "But witches have gone out of style, haven't they?"

Bill had had a run-in with Addie Fitch the month before. He had hit her cat with his car and killed it. "I'm really sorry, Addie Fitch," he told her. "I'll get you a new cat, just as pretty, just as good."

Her eyes filled with hate. "I raised that cat from a kitten," she hissed. "I loved her. You'll be sorry for this, Bill Nelson."

Bill sent her a new cat and heard nothing more.

Then his cow stopped giving milk. Next his old truck broke down. After that, his wife fell and broke her arm. "We're having a lot of bad luck," he thought. Then he thought, "Maybe it is Addie Fitch gettin' even." And then, "Hey—you don't believe in witches. You're just upset."

But Bill's grandpa believed in witches. He had once told Bill that there was only one sure way to stop a witch from causing trouble. "You find a black walnut tree," he said, "and you draw her picture on it. Then you mark an X where her heart is, and you drive a nail into the X. Every day you drive it in a little deeper.

"If she's causing the trouble," he said, "she'll feel pain. When she can't stand it anymore, she'll come to you, or send somebody, and try to borrow something. If you give her what she wants, that breaks the power of the nail, and she'll go on tormenting you. But if you don't, she'll have to stop—or the pain will kill her."

That's what his nice, gentle old grandpa believed. "It's pure craziness," Bill thought. Of course, his grandpa didn't have much schooling. Bill had been to college. He knew better.

Then Bill's dog Joe, a perfectly healthy dog, dropped dead, just like that. It made Bill angry. Despite all his schooling, he thought, "Maybe it is Addie Fitch after all."

He got a red crayon from his son's room, and a hammer and a nail, and went into the woods. He found a black walnut tree and drew a picture of Addie Fitch on it. He made an *X* where her heart was, like his grandpa had said to do. With the hammer he drove the nail a little way into the *X*. Then he went home.

"I feel like a fool," he told his wife.

"You should," she said.

The next day a boy named Timmy Logan came by. "Addie Fitch isn't feeling well," he said. "She wonders if she could borrow some sugar from you."

Bill Nelson stared at Timmy in amazement. He took a deep breath. "Tell her I'm sorry, but I don't have any sugar right now," he said.

When Timmy Logan left, Bill went back to the walnut tree and drove the nail in another inch. The next day the boy came back. "Addie Fitch is pretty sick," he said. "She's wondering if you've got any sugar yet."

"Tell her I'm sorry," Bill Nelson said. "But I still don't have any."

Bill went out into the woods and drove the nail in another inch. The following day the boy was back. "Addie Fitch is getting sicker," he said. "She really needs some sugar."

"Tell her I still don't have any," Bill answered.

Bill's wife was angry. "You've got to stop this," she said. "If this mumbo jumbo works, it's like murder."

"I'll stop when she does," he said.

Toward dusk he stood in the yard staring at the ridge where the old lady lived, wondering what was going on up there. Then, in the half darkness, he saw Addie Fitch coming slowly down the hill toward him. With her

pinched, bony face and her old black coat, she did look like a witch. As she got closer, Bill saw that she could barely walk.

"Maybe I'm really hurting her," he thought. He ran to get his hammer to pull the nail out. But before he could leave, Addie Fitch was in the yard, her face twisted with rage.

"First you killed my cat," she said. "Then you wouldn't give me a bit of sugar when I needed it." She swore at him, and fell dead at his feet.

*

"I'm not surprised that she dropped dead that way," the doctor said later. "She was very old, maybe ninety. It was her heart, of course."

"Some people thought she was a witch," Bill said.

"I've heard that," the doctor said.

"Somebody I know thought Addie Fitch had witched him," Bill went on. "He drew a picture of her on a tree, then drove a nail into it to make her stop."

"That's an old superstition," the doctor said. "But people like us don't believe in that sort of thing, do we?"

Running Wild

A young child is stolen by wild animals.
For some reason
the animals raise the child instead of eating it.
It learns to make the sounds they make.
It learns to eat, run, and kill
the way they do.
After a while it only <u>looks</u> human.

· *THE WOLF GIRL* ·

Travel northwest into the desert from Del Rio, Texas, and eventually you will come to Devil's River. In the 1830s a trapper named John Dent and his wife Mollie settled where Dry Creek runs into Devil's River. Dent was after beaver, which were plentiful there. He and Mollie built a cabin from brush, and near it they put up an arbor to give them shade.

Mollie Dent became pregnant. When she was ready to have their child, John Dent raced on horseback to their nearest neighbors, several miles away.

"My wife is having a baby," he said to the man and his wife. "Can you help us?" They agreed to come at once. As they got ready to leave, a violent storm came up and a bolt of lightning struck and killed John Dent. The man and his wife managed to find his cabin, but did not arrive until the next day. By then Mollie Dent was dead, too.

It looked as if she had given birth before she died, but the neighbors could not find the baby. Since there were wolf tracks all around, they decided the wolves had eaten it. They buried Mollie Dent and left.

A number of years after she died, people began to tell a strange tale. Some swore it was a true story. Others said it never could have happened.

*

The story begins in a small settlement a dozen miles from Mollie Dent's grave. Early one morning a pack of wolves raced in from the desert and killed some goats. Such attacks were not unusual in those days. But a boy thought he saw a naked young girl with long blond hair running with the wolves.

A year or two later, a woman came upon some wolves eating a goat they had just killed. Eating the goat with them, she claimed, was a naked young girl with long blond hair. When the wolves and the girl saw her, they fled. The woman said that at first the girl ran on all fours. Then she stood and ran like a human, swiftly as the wolves.

People started wondering if this "wolf girl" was Mollie Dent's daughter. Had a mother wolf carried her off the day she was born and raised her with her pups? If so, by now she would be ten or eleven years old.

As the story is told, some men began to look for the girl. They searched along the riverbanks and in the desert and its canyons. And one day, it is said, they found her, walking in a canyon with a wolf at her side. When the wolf ran off, the girl hid in an opening in one of the canyon walls.

When the men tried to capture her, she fought back, biting and scratching like an enraged animal. When they finally subdued her, she began screaming like a frightened young girl and howling like a frightened young wolf.

Her captors bound her with rope, put her across a horse, and took her to a small ranch house in the desert. They would turn her over to the sheriff the next day, they decided. They placed her in an empty room and untied her. Terror-stricken, she hid in the shadows. They left her and locked the door.

Soon she was screaming and howling again. The men thought they would go mad listening to her, but at last she stopped. When night fell, wolves began howling in the

distance. People say that each time they stopped, the girl howled in reply.

As the story goes, the cries of wolves came from every direction and got closer and closer. Suddenly, as if a signal had been given, wolves attacked the horses and other livestock. The men rushed into the darkness, firing their guns.

High up in the wall, in the room where they had left the girl, was a small window. A plank was nailed across it. She pulled the plank off, crawled through the window, and disappeared.

*

Years passed with no word of the girl. Then one day some men on horseback came around a bend in the Rio Grande not far from Devil's River. They claimed they saw a young woman with long blond hair feeding two wolf pups.

When she saw the men, she snatched up the pups and ran into the brush. They rode after her, but she quickly left them behind. They searched and searched, but found no trace of her. That is the last we know of the wolf girl. And it is there, in the desert, near the Rio Grande, that this story ends.

Five Nightmares

An artist painted some pictures.
A boy got a new pet.
A girl went on vacation.
Everything was normal.
Then nothing was.

· THE DREAM ·

Lucy Morgan was an artist. She had spent a week painting in a small country town and decided that the next day she would move on. She would go to a village called Kingston.

But that night Lucy Morgan had a strange dream. She dreamed that she was walking up a dark, carved staircase and entered a bedroom. It was an ordinary room except for two things. The carpet was made up of large squares that looked like trapdoors. And each of the windows was fastened shut with big nails that stuck up out of the wood.

In her dream Lucy Morgan went to sleep in that bedroom. During the night a woman with a pale face and black eyes and long black hair came into the room. She leaned over the bed and whispered, "This is an evil place. Flee while you can." When the woman touched her arm to hurry her along, Lucy Morgan awakened from her dream with a shriek. She lay awake the rest of the night trembling.

In the morning she told her landlady that she had decided not to go to Kingston after all. "I can't tell you why," she said, "but I just can't bring myself to go there."

"Then why don't you go to Dorset?" the landlady said. "It's a pretty town, and it isn't too far."

So Lucy Morgan went to Dorset. Someone told her she could find a room in a house at the top of the hill. It was a pleasant-looking house, and the landlady there, a plump, motherly woman, was as nice as could be. "Let's look at the room," she said. "I think you will like it."

They walked up a dark, carved staircase, like the one in Lucy's dream. "In these old houses the staircases are all the same," Lucy thought. But when the landlady opened the door to the bedroom, it was the room in her dream, with the same carpet that looked like trapdoors and the same windows fastened with big nails.

"This is just a coincidence," Lucy told herself.

"How do you like it?" the landlady asked.

"I'm not sure," she said.

"Well, take your time," the landlady said. "I'll bring up some tea while you think about it."

Lucy sat on the bed staring at the trapdoors and the big nails. Soon there was a knock on the door. "It's the land-lady with tea," she thought.

But it wasn't the landlady. It was the woman with the pale face and the black eyes and the long black hair. Lucy Morgan grabbed her things and fled.

· SAM'S NEW PET ·

Sam stayed with his grandmother when his parents went to Mexico for their vacation. "We are going to bring you back something nice," his mother told him. "It will be a surprise."

Before they came home, Sam's parents looked for something Sam would like. All they could find was a beautiful sombrero. It cost too much. But that afternoon, while they were eating their lunch in a park, they decided to buy the sombrero after all. Sam's father threw what was left of their sandwiches to some stray dogs, and they walked back to the marketplace.

One of the animals followed them. It was a small, gray creature with short hair, short legs, and a long tail. Wherever they went, it went.

"Isn't he cute!" Sam's mother said. "He must be one of those Mexican Hairless dogs. Sam would love him."

"He's probably somebody's pet," Sam's father said.

They asked several people if they knew who its owners were, but no one did. They just smiled and shrugged their shoulders. Finally, Sam's mother said, "Maybe he's just a stray. Let's take him home with us. We can give him a good home, and Sam will love him."

It is against the law to take a pet across the border, but Sam's parents hid the animal in a box, and no one saw it. When they got home, they showed it to Sam.

"He's a pretty small dog," said Sam.

"He's a Mexican dog," his father said. "I'm not sure what kind. I think it's called a Mexican Hairless. We'll find out. But he's nice, isn't he?"

They gave the new pet some dog food. Then they washed it and brushed it and combed its fur. That night it slept on Sam's bed. When Sam awakened the next morning, his pet was still there.

"Mother," he called, "the dog has a cold." The animal's eyes were running, and there was something white around its mouth. Later that morning Sam's mother took it to a veterinarian.

"Where did you get him?" the vet asked.

"In Mexico," she said. "We think he's a Mexican Hairless. I was going to ask you about that."

"He's not a Hairless," the vet said. "He's not even a dog. He's a sewer rat—and he has rabies."

· *MAYBE YOU WILL REMEMBER* ·

Mrs. Gibbs and her sixteen-year-old daughter Rosemary arrived in Paris on a hot morning in July. They had been on a vacation and now were returning home. But Mrs. Gibbs did not feel well. So they decided to rest in Paris for a few days before going on.

The city was crowded with tourists. Still, they found a place to stay at a good hotel. They had a lovely room overlooking a park. It had yellow walls, a blue carpet, and white furniture.

As soon as they unpacked, Mrs. Gibbs went to bed. She looked so pale that Rosemary asked to have the hotel's doctor examine her. Rosemary did not speak French, but fortunately the doctor spoke English.

He took one look at Mrs. Gibbs and said, "Your mother is too sick to travel. Tomorrow I will move her to a hospital, but she needs a certain medicine. If you go to my home for it, it will save time." The doctor said he did not have a telephone right now. Instead, he would give Rosemary a note for his wife.

The hotel manager put Rosemary in a taxi and, in French, told the driver how to find the doctor's house. "It will take only a little while," he told her, "and the taxi will bring you back." But as the driver slowly drove up one street and down another, it seemed to take forever. At one point Rosemary was sure they had gone down the same street twice.

It took almost as long for the doctor's wife to answer the door, then get the medicine ready. As Rosemary sat on a bench in the empty waiting room, she kept thinking, "Why can't you hurry? Please hurry." Then she heard a telephone ring somewhere in the house. But the doctor had told her he didn't have a telephone right now. What was going on?

They drove back as slowly as they had come, crawling up one street and down another. Rosemary sat in the backseat filled with dread, her mother's medicine clutched in her hand. Why was everything taking so long?

She was sure the taxi driver was going in the wrong direction. "Are you going to the right hotel?" she asked. He didn't answer. She asked again, but still he didn't reply. When he stopped for a traffic light, she threw open the door and ran from the cab.

She stopped a woman on the street. The woman did not speak English, but she knew someone who did. Rosemary was right. They *had* been driving in the wrong direction.

When she finally got back to the hotel, it was early evening. She went up to the desk clerk who had given

them their room. "I'm Rosemary Gibbs," she said. "My mother and I are in Room 505. May I please have the key?"

The clerk looked at her closely. "You must be mistaken," he said. "There is another guest in that room. Are you sure you are in the right hotel?" He turned to help someone else. She waited until he was finished.

"You gave us that room yourself when we arrived this morning," she said. "How could you forget?"

He stared at her as if she had lost her mind. "You must be mistaken," he said. "I have never seen you before. Are you sure you are in the right hotel?"

She asked to see the registration card they had filled out when they arrived. "It's June and Rosemary Gibbs," she said.

The clerk looked in the file. "We have no card for you," he said. "You must be in the wrong hotel."

"The hotel doctor will know me," Rosemary replied. "He examined my mother when we arrived. He sent me for medicine she needs. I want to see him."

The doctor came downstairs. "Here is the medicine for my mother," Rosemary said, holding it out to him. "Your wife gave it to me."

"I have never seen you before," he said. "You must be in the wrong hotel."

She asked for the hotel manager who had put her in the taxi. Surely he would remember her. "You must be in the wrong hotel," he said. "Let me give you a room where you can rest. Then maybe you will remember where you and your mother are staying."

"I want to see our room!" Rosemary said, raising her

voice. "It's Room 505."

But it was nothing like the room she remembered. It had a double bed, not twin beds. The furniture was black, not white. The carpet was green, not blue. There was someone else's clothing in the closet. The room she knew had vanished. And so had her mother.

"This is not the room," she said. "Where is my mother? What have you done with her?"

"You are in the wrong hotel," the manager said patiently, as if he were speaking to a young child.

Rosemary asked to see the police. "My mother, our things, the room, they have all disappeared," she told them.

"Are you sure you are in the right hotel?" they asked.

She went to her embassy for help. "Are you sure it is the right hotel?" they asked.

Rosemary thought that she was losing her mind.

"Why don't you rest here for a while," they said. "Then maybe you'll remember..."

*

But Rosemary's problem was not her memory. It was what she did not know. See page 102.

· *THE RED SPOT* ·

While Ruth slept, a spider crawled across her face. It stopped for several minutes on her left cheek, then went on its way.

"What is that red spot on my cheek?" she asked her mother the next morning.

"It looks like a spider bite," her mother said. "It will go away. Just don't scratch it."

Soon the small red spot grew into a small red boil. "Look at it now," Ruth said. "It's getting bigger. It's sore."

"That sometimes happens," her mother said. "It's coming to a head."

In a few days the boil was even larger. "Look at it now," Ruth said. "It hurts and it's ugly."

"We'll have the doctor look at it," her mother said. "Maybe it's infected." But the doctor could not see Ruth until the next day.

That night Ruth took a hot bath. As she soaked herself, the boil burst. Out poured a swarm of tiny spiders from the eggs their mother had laid in her cheek.

· *NO, THANKS* ·

Thursday nights Jim worked as a stock boy in one of the malls out on the highway. By eight-thirty he was usually finished and he drove home.

But that night Jim was one of the last to leave. By the time he got out to the huge parking lot, it was almost empty. The only sounds were cars in the distance and his footsteps on the pavement.

Suddenly a man stepped out of the shadows. "Hey, mister," he called in a low voice. He held out his right hand. Balanced on the palm was the long, thin blade of a knife.

Jim stopped.

"Nice, sharp knife," the man said softly.

"Don't panic," Jim thought.

The man stepped toward him.

"Don't run," Jim told himself.

"Nice, sharp knife," the man repeated.

"Give him what he wants," Jim thought.

The man came closer. He held the knife up. "Cuts nice and easy," he said slowly. Jim waited. The man peered into his face. "Hey, man, only three dollars. Two for five. Nice present for your mama."

"No, thanks," Jim said. "She's got one." And he ran for his car.

What Is Going On Here?

When bottles began popping
and furniture began flying all over the house,
there were many explanations.
but none of them was right.
Then someone had a scary answer
that could involve you.

· THE TROUBLE ·

The events in this story took place in 1958 in a small white house in a suburb of New York City. The names of the people involved have been changed.

*

Monday, February 3. Tom Lombardo and his sister Nancy had just come home from school. Tom was going on thirteen. Nancy was fourteen. They were talking to their mother in the living room when they heard a loud POP! in the kitchen. It sounded like a cork had been pulled from a bottle of champagne.

But it was nothing like that. The cap on a bottle of starch had somehow come unscrewed, and the bottle had tipped over and spilled. Then bottles all over the house began popping—bottles of nail polish remover, shampoo, bleach, rubbing alcohol, even a bottle of holy water.

Each had a screw cap that took two or three full turns to open. But each had opened *by itself*—without any human help—then had fallen over and spilled.

"What is going on here?" Mrs. Lombardo asked. Nobody knew. But the popping soon stopped and everything went back to normal. It was just one of those crazy things, they decided, and put it out of their minds.

Thursday, February 6. Just after Tom and Nancy got home from school, six more bottles popped their caps. The next day, at about the same time, another six did.

Sunday, February 9. At eleven o'clock that morning Tom was in the bathroom brushing his teeth. His father was standing in the doorway talking to him. All of a sudden a bottle of medicine began moving across the vanity by it-self and fell into the sink. At the same time a bottle of shampoo moved to the edge of the vanity and crashed to the floor. They watched, spellbound.

"I'd better call the police," Mr. Lombardo said. That afternoon a patrolman interviewed the family as bottles popped in the bathroom. The police assigned a detective named Joseph Briggs to the case.

Detective Briggs was a practical man. When something moved, he believed that a human or an animal had moved it, or that it moved because of a vibration or the wind or some other natural cause. He did not believe in ghosts.

When the Lombardos said they had nothing to do with what was going on, he thought that at least one of them was lying. He wanted to examine the house. Then he wanted to talk to some experts and find out what they thought.

Tuesday, February 11. The bottle of holy water that had opened a week before opened a second time and spilled. Two days later it spilled again.

Saturday, February 15. Tom, Nancy, and a relative were watching TV in the living room when a small porcelain statue rose up from a table. It flew three feet through the air, then fell to the rug.

Monday, February 17. A priest blessed the Lombardos' house to protect it against whatever was causing the trouble.

Thursday, February 20. While Tom was doing his homework at one end of the dining room table, a sugar bowl at the other end flew into the hall and crashed. Detective

Briggs saw it happen. Later a bottle of ink on the table flew into a wall and broke, spattering in all directions. Then another porcelain statue took off. It traveled twelve feet and smashed into a desk.

Friday, February 21. To get some peace, the Lombardos went to a relative's house for the weekend. While they were gone, everything at home was normal.

Sunday, February 23. When the Lombardos returned, another sugar bowl took off. It flew into a wall and smashed to smithereens. Later a heavy bureau in Tom's room toppled over. But no one was in the room when it happened.

Monday, February 24. By now Detective Briggs had talked to an engineer, a chemist, a physicist, and others. Some thought that vibrations in the house were causing the trouble. These could come from underground water, they said, or from high-frequency radio waves, or from sonic booms caused by airplanes. Others said that the electrical system was the cause, or downdrafts coming through the chimney. The popping of bottles was blamed on chemicals the bottles contained.

Tests showed that there were no vibrations in the house; there was nothing wrong with the electrical system; and there were no chemicals in the bottles that would make them pop.

Then *what* was causing the trouble? None of the experts knew. But every day the Lombardos received dozens of letters and telephone calls from people who thought they did know. Many believed that the house was haunted. They thought that a poltergeist was on the loose—the

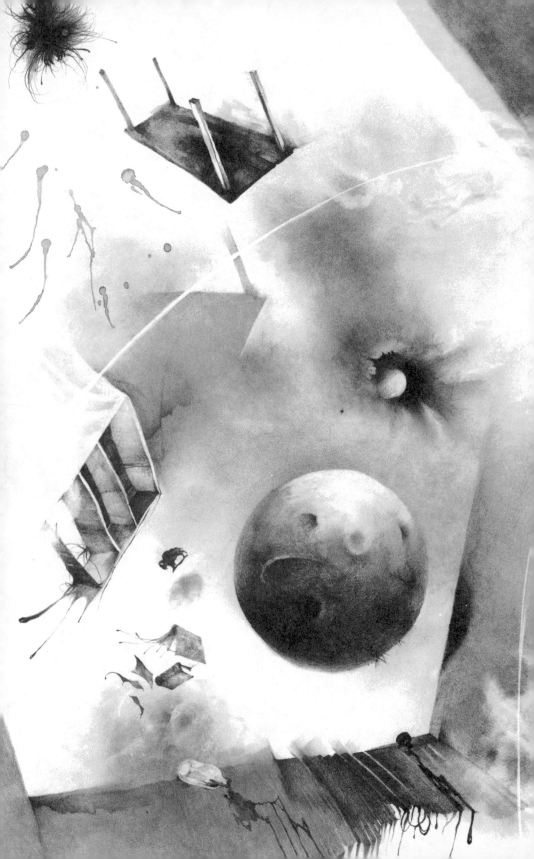

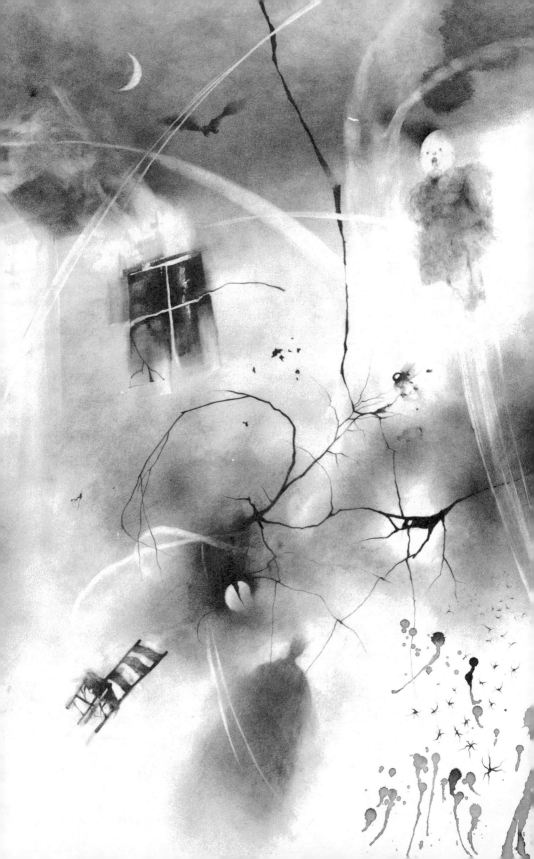

noisy ghost that is blamed when things move around on their own.

No one has proved that poltergeists exist. But people everywhere have told stories about them for hundreds of years. And what they have told was not too different from what was happening to the Lombardos.

Detective Briggs did not, of course, believe in poltergeists. He had begun to believe that Tom Lombardo might be to blame. Whenever something happened, Tom was usually in the room or nearby. When he accused Tom of causing the trouble, the boy denied it. "I don't know what's going on," he said. "All I know is that it scares me."

People said that Detective Briggs was a tough cop who would turn in his mother if she did something wrong. But he believed Tom. Only now he didn't know what to think.

Tuesday, February 25. A newspaper reporter came to the house to interview the family. Afterward he sat in the living room by himself hoping that something would happen that he could describe in his story.

Tom's room was just across the hall from where the reporter sat. The boy had gone to bed, but he had left his door open. Suddenly a globe of the world flew out of the darkened room and smashed into a wall. The reporter dashed into the bedroom and turned on the light. Tom was sitting in bed blinking, as if he had just been awakened from a sound sleep. "What was that?" he asked.

Wednesday, February 26. In the morning a small plastic statue of the Virgin Mary rose up from a dresser in Mr. and Mrs. Lombardo's bedroom and flew into a mirror. That night, while Tom was doing his homework, a ten-pound record player took off from a table, flew fifteen feet, then crashed to the floor.

Friday, February 28. Two scientists arrived from Duke University in North Carolina. They were parapsychologists who studied experiences like those the Lombardos were having. They spent several days talking to the family and examining the house, trying to understand what was going on and what was causing it. One night a bottle of bleach popped its top, but that was all that happened during their visit.

They did not tell the Lombardos about a theory they had that a poltergeist actually might be involved in such cases. According to this idea, poltergeists were not ghosts. They were normal teenagers. They had become so troubled by a problem that their emotions built up into a kind of vibration. Since it was taking place in their unconscious minds, they didn't even know it was happening. But the vibration somehow left their bodies and moved whatever it struck. It happened again and again until the problem had been solved.

Scientists had given this strange power a name. They called it "psychokinesis," the ability to move objects with mental power, or mind over matter. No one knew if this really could happen, or how to prove it. Yet most reports of poltergeists did involve families with teenage children, and there were two teenagers in the Lombardo family.

Monday, March 3. The parapsychologists said that they would prepare a report on what they had learned. The day after they left the trouble returned with a vengeance.

Tuesday, March 4. In the afternoon a bowl of flowers flew

off the dining-room table and smashed into a cupboard. Then a bottle of bleach jumped out of a cardboard box and popped its top. Then a bookcase filled with encyclopedias fell over and wedged itself between a radiator and a wall. Then a flashlight bulb on a table rose up and hit a wall twelve feet away. Finally, four knocks were heard coming from the kitchen when nobody was in that room.

Wednesday, March 5. While Mrs. Lombardo was making breakfast, she heard a loud crash in the living room. The coffee table had turned over by itself. But that was the end of it. After a month of chaos everything returned to normal.

*

In August the two parapsychologists gave their report. They decided that the Lombardos had not made up the story. Nor had they imagined it. Their trouble had been real. But what had caused it?

They said that no pranks or tricks were involved, nor was any magic. As the police had done, they also ruled out vibrations from underground water and other physical causes.

The only explanation they could not rule out was the possibility that a teenage poltergeist had been at work, moving objects with mental power. They did not have enough evidence to prove it, but it was the only answer they had.

If it was a poltergeist, they thought it was Tom. If they were right, if a normal boy like Tom had become a poltergeist, this also might happen to other teenagers. It might even happen to you.

Whoooooooo?

There are four ghosts,
a ghostly monster,
and a corpse in this chapter.
But the stories about them
are funny,
not scary.

· STRANGERS ·

A man and a woman happened to sit next to one another on a train. The woman took out a book and began reading. The train stopped at a half dozen stations, but she never looked up once.

The man watched her for a while, then asked, "What are you reading?"

"It's a ghost story," she said. "It's very good, *very* spooky."

"Do you believe in ghosts?" he asked.

"Yes, I do," she replied. "There are ghosts everywhere."

"I don't believe in them," he said. "It's just a lot of superstition. In all my years I've never seen a ghost, not one."

"Haven't you?" the woman said—and vanished.

· *THE HOG* ·

When Arthur and Anne were in high school, they fell in love. They were both big, fat, and jolly and seemed suited to one another. But as sometimes happens, things didn't work out.

Arthur moved away and married someone else, and Anne didn't marry anyone. And not too many years later, she got sick and died. Some said it was from a broken heart.

One day Arthur was driving to a small town not far from where he and Anne had grown up. Soon he realized that a hog was following him. No matter how fast Arthur drove, the hog stayed right behind. Each time he looked back, there was the hog. It began to irritate him.

Finally he couldn't stand it any longer. He stopped his car and rapped the hog on its snout good and hard. "Get out of here, you fat, dirty thing!" he shouted.

To his astonishment, the hog spoke to him, and it was Anne's voice he heard. "It's her ghost!" he thought. "She has come back as a hog!"

"I was doing no harm, Arthur," the hog said. "I was just out for a brisk walk, enjoying myself. How could you strike me after all that we meant to one another?" With that, she turned and trotted away .

*

(When you tell this story, have the hog speak in a high voice.)

· IS SOMETHING WRONG? ·

A car broke down late at night way out in the country. The driver remembered passing an empty house a few minutes earlier. "I'll stay there," he thought. "At least I'll get some sleep."

He found some wood in the corner of the living room and made a fire in the fireplace. He covered himself with his coat and slept. Toward morning the fire went out, and the cold awakened him. "It'll be light soon," he thought. "Then I'll go for help."

He closed his eyes again. But before he could doze off there was a terrible crash. Something big and heavy had fallen out of the chimney. It lay on the floor for a minute. Then it stood up and stared down at him.

The man took one look and started running. He had never seen anything so horrible in his life. He paused just long enough to jump through a window. Then he ran, and ran, and ran—and ran until he thought his lungs would burst.

As he stood in the road panting, trying to catch his breath, he felt something tap him on the shoulder. He turned and found himself staring into two big, bloody eyes in a grinning skull. It was the horrible thing!

"Pardon me," it said. "Is something wrong?"

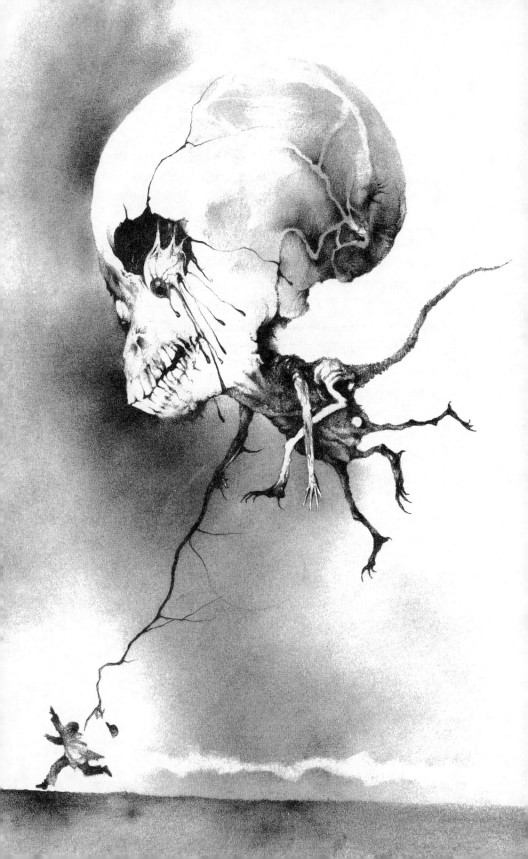

· IT'S _HIM!_ ·

The woman was the meanest, most miserable person you could imagine. And her husband was just as bad. The only good thing was that they lived in the woods all by themselves and couldn't bother anybody else.

One day they were off somewhere getting firewood, and the woman got so mad at her husband that she grabbed an ax and cut his head off, just like that. Then she buried him nice and neat and went home.

She made herself a cup of tea and went out on the porch. She sat there rocking in her rocking chair, sipping her tea, thinking how glad she was that she had done this awful thing. After a while she heard this old, empty voice out in the distance moaning and groaning, and it was saying:

"Whooooooooo's going to stay with me this cold and lonely night? Whoooooooo?"

"It's _him!_" she thought. And she hollered back, "Stay by yourself, you old goat."

Soon she heard the voice again, only now it was closer, and it was saying:

"Whoooooooo's going to sit with me this cold and lonely night? Whoooooooo?"

"Only a crazy man!" she shouted. "Sit by yourself, you dirty rat!"

Then she heard the voice even closer, and it was saying:

"Whoooooooo's going to be with me this cold and lonely night? Whoooooooo?"

"Nobody!" she sneered. "Be by yourself, you miserable mole!"

She stood up to go into the house, but now the voice was right behind her, and it was whispering:

"Whoooooooo's going to stay with me this cold and lonely night? Whoooooooo?"

Before she could answer back, a big hairy hand came around the corner and grabbed her, and the voice hollered:

"*YOU* ARE!"

*

(As you say the last line, grab one of your friends.)

· T-H-U-P-P-P-P-P-P-P! ·

After Sarah went to bed, she saw a ghost. It was sitting on her dresser staring at her through two black holes where its eyes had been. She shrieked, and her mother and father came running.

"There's a ghost on my dresser," she said, trembling. "It's staring at me."

When they turned on the light, it was gone. "You were having a bad dream," her father said. "Now go to sleep."

But after they left, there it was again, sitting on her dresser staring at her. She pulled the blanket over her head and fell asleep.

The next night the ghost was back. It was up on the ceiling staring down at her. When Sarah saw it, she screamed. Again her mother and father came running.

"It's up on the ceiling," she said.

When they turned on the light, nothing was there. "It's your imagination," her mother said, and gave her a hug.

But after they left, there it was again, staring down at her from the ceiling. She put her head under the pillow and fell asleep.

The next night the ghost was back. It was sitting on her bed staring at her. Sarah called to her parents, and they came running.

"It's on my bed," she said. "It's looking and looking at me."

When they turned on the light, nothing was there. "You're upset over nothing," her father said. He kissed her on the nose and tucked her in. "Now go to sleep."

But after they left, there it was again, sitting on her bed staring at her.

"Why are you doing this to me?" Sarah asked. "Why don't you leave me alone?"

The ghost put its fingers in its ears and wiggled them at her. Then it stuck its tongue out and went:

"T-H-U-P-P-P-P-P-P-P!"

*

(To make this sound, put your tongue between your lips and blow. It is called giving someone "the raspberry.")

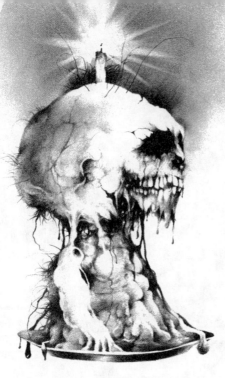

· *YOU MAY BE THE NEXT . . .* ·

Did you ev - er think as a hearse goes by, that

you may be___ the next to die?

Did you ever think as a hearse goes by
That you may be the next to die?
They wrap you up in a big white sheet
From your head down to your feet.
And the worms crawl in and the worms crawl out,
In your stomach and out your snout,
And your eyes fall out and your teeth decay—
And that is the end of a perfect day.

NOTES and SOURCES

BIBLIOGRAPHY

ACKNOWLEDGMENTS

Notes and Sources

The sources given are described in the Bibliography.

BOO MEN

"Boo men" is a name for imaginary scary creatures in Newfoundland. Boo men are similar to bogarts in Great Britain, from where many Newfoundlanders came, and to bogey men and boogeymen in America. See Widdowson, *If You Don't Be Good*, pp. 157–60; Widdowson, "The Bogeyman."

The story about the girl who meets a ghost in a cemetery is told in many places.

WHEN DEATH ARRIVES

The Appointment: This story is the retelling of an ancient tale that is usually set in Asia. A young man sees Death in the marketplace in Damascus, the capital of Syria. To escape his fate, he flees to either Baghdad or Samarra in what is now Iraq. Death is, of course, waiting for him. In some versions, Death is a woman, not a man. The story has been told in one form or another by Edith Wharton, the English author W. Somerset Maugham, and the French writer Jean Cocteau. The American novelist John O'Hara entitled his first book *An Appointment in Samarra*. See Woollcott, pp. 602–3.

The Bus Stop: This is from the family of "vanishing hitchhiker" stories in which a ghost returns in human form. It usually is seen on a street corner late at night or during a storm and is offered a ride home in a car. But when the driver arrives at his destination, the passenger has disappeared. In the story "The Bus Stop," the ghost remains in human form for several weeks before disappearing.

The story is based on several versions. One is a recollection by Barbara Carmer Schwartz from the 1940s in Delmar, New York. There also is a version in which the young man loses his mind when he learns that the young woman is a ghost. See Jones, *Things That Go Bump in the Night*, pp. 173–74.

A similar story was told in ancient Rome. It involved a young woman named Philinnion who died, then six months later was seen with a man she loved who did not know of her death. When her parents learn of her appearance, they rush to see her. She accuses them of interfering in her "life," then dies a second time. See Collison-Morley, pp. 652–72.

The folklorist Jan Brunvand lists many variants of the vanishing hitchhiker tale in *The Vanishing Hitchhiker*, pp. 24–40, 41–46.

There also have been at least two popular songs on the subject: "Laurie (Strange Things Happen)," a pop-rock song of the early 1960s composed by Milton C. Addington, and "Bringing Mary Home," a bluegrass song composed in 1961 by Joe Kingston and M. K. Scosa. Both were still being performed when this book was written.

Faster and Faster: This is retold from a summer-camp story of the 1940s in New York or New Hampshire. Ruth L. Tongue prints an account she collected in 1964 in Berkshire, England, in which some city boys find an old hunting horn in Windsor Forest. When one of them blows it, he summons up the ghosts of a hunting party and is killed by the ghostly arrows of a ghostly hunter. See Tongue, p. 52.

Just Delicious: This is one of hundreds of stories that make up what folklorists call the "Man from the Gallows" family, or tale type 366. They are found in America, Great Britain, Western Europe, and parts of Africa and Asia. Perhaps the best known in the English-speaking world is "The Man with the Golden Arm." For a version, see

Schwartz, *Tomfoolery,* pp. 28–30.

Such stories have their roots in the ancient tale of the man with no work whose family was starving. Searching for food, he comes to a gallows where a criminal has just been hanged. He cuts out the dead man's heart (or some other part of his body) and takes it home. That night his family feasts. But while they sleep, the man from the gallows comes looking for the part of his body that had been stolen. When he cannot find it, he takes with him the person who stole it. See Thompson, *The Folktale,* p. 42.

"Just Delicious" is a story that closely follows this tale. The retelling is based on accounts I have heard over the years in the northeastern United States, the earliest in the 1940s. Louis C. Jones prints a New York City version in which the husband saves himself by removing his wife's liver and giving it to the ghost as a substitute for the one she had stolen. See Jones, *Things That Go Bump in the Night,* pp. 96–99.

Hello, Kate!: This story is based on a legend from southwest Munster, Ireland. See Curtin, pp. 59–60.

The Black Dog: The story is based on an experience reported in the French village of Bourg-en-Forêt in the 1920s. A spectral black dog like the one in this story is said to be the ghost of a wicked human or a foreteller of death. See Van Paassen, pp. 246–50.

Footsteps: This story is loosely based on one collected in Amherst, Nova Scotia, by the Canadian folklorist Helen Creighton. See Creighton, pp. 264–66.

Like Cats' Eyes: This is adapted from a story the English author Augustus Hare was told in the late nineteenth century. In that version the hearse was pulled by four horses. See Hare, pp. 49–50.

ON THE EDGE

Bess: This story is based on an old European legend. The Swiss folklorist Max Lüthi named it "Oleg's Death" for the ruler Oleg, who lived almost two thousand years ago in what today is Russia. He is said to have died as John Nicholas did in our story, bitten by a poisonous snake hiding in the remains of a horse he feared.

The legend contains many themes that are frequently found in folk literature: What seems weak may be strong, what seems impossible may be possible, the greatest danger we face is from ourselves. See Lüthi, "Parallel Themes."

Harold: Several tales in folklore and fiction tell of a doll or some other figure a person creates that comes to life. In the Jewish legend of the golem, a rabbi uses a charm to give life to a clay statue. When it goes out of control, he destroys it. In Mary Wollstonecraft Shelley's novel *Frankenstein*, a Swiss student discovers how to bring lifeless matter alive and is destroyed by the monster he creates.

In the Greek fairy tale "The Gentleman Made of Groats," or "Mr. Simigaldi," a princess cannot find herself a good husband. So she creates one by mixing a kilo of almonds, a kilo of sugar, and a kilo of groats, which is similar to grits, and gives the mixture the shape of a man. In answer to her prayers, God gives the figure life. After many adventures, the two live happily.

The story "Harold" is retold from an Austrian-Swiss legend. See Lüthi, *Once Upon a Time*, pp. 83–87.

The Dead Hand: This legend was told in Lincolnshire in eastern England in the nineteenth century. It takes place in the Lincolnshire Cars, then a vast marshland on the North Sea that local people believed was a home to evil spirits. The story is shortened and adapted from M. C. Balfour, pp. 271–78.

Such Things Happen: This is a traditional American legend in which a person believes he is being tormented by a witch and tries to stop her. In some stories the person tries to kill the witch by drawing her picture and firing a silver bullet into it or by hammering a nail into it. I adapted and expanded this theme to point up the conflict between education and superstition that may arise when an educated person feels that events are out of control. See in Thompson, "Granny Frone," *Folk Tales and Legends*, pp. 650–52; Cox, pp. 208–9; Randolph, *Ozark Magic*, pp. 288–90; Yarborough, p. 97.

RUNNING WILD

The Wolf Girl: This legend from southwest Texas about a child who grew up wild is similar to stories found in many cultures. Some are described below.

I first heard about the Texas wolf girl in 1975 while in El Paso doing research for another book. A retired laborer then in his eighties, Juan de la Cruz Machuca, told me the story as he knew it. His version overlaps the account in "The Lobo Girl of Devil's River," an article on the history of the incident by L. D. Bertillion, that appeared in 1937. See Bertillion, pp. 79–85. My retelling is drawn from oral accounts and that article.

Bertillion begins his story when the trapper Dent falls in love with Mollie Pertul in Georgia, then soon after kills his partner in a trapping business and escapes. A year later he returns for Mollie and the two steal away to Texas and settle on Devil's River. There Mollie gives birth to their child who, in legend, became known as the wolf girl.

Sections of Devil's River and the Rio Grande where the wolf girl is said to have roamed have in modern times been flooded for a reservoir and recreation area.

One of the oldest legends of children who are raised by wolves is the famous story of the newborn twins Romulus and Remus, whose mother was said to have set them afloat in a basket on the Tiber River in ancient Latium. When the basket washed ashore, the boys were suckled by a she-wolf until a shepherd came upon them and raised them. In legend, Romulus founded Rome where the twins had been rescued from the Tiber.

In the story "Mowgli's Brother," Rudyard Kipling writes of a baby boy in India who walked into a den of wolves and was raised by them. See Kipling, pp. 1–43.

A modern legend from the Ozark Mountains in Arkansas tells of a five-month-old boy who disappeared when his mother placed him on the ground while she was hoeing corn with her husband. Years later some person or animal began stealing chickens from their farm, but the couple could not put a stop to it. One night the husband saw a naked boy run off with a chicken. When he followed the boy to a cave, he found him with an old, sick she-wolf that was eating the chicken. The boy growled at the farmer like a wolf, but the farmer managed to carry him off. It was, of course, his son. See Parler, p. 4.

There also are stories about young people who grew up wild after their parents had abandoned them, or after they had gotten lost or had been cast away. One is the true story of the wild boy of Aveyron who lived on his own in the wilderness in southern France from about 1795 to 1800, when he was captured. See Shattuck.

There are two California legends of such cases. One involves a two-year-old girl who washed ashore on an island off Santa Barbara after a sailboat swamped in the early 1900s. Years later men hunting wild goats on the island came upon a young woman who bounded away like a goat. They found her cowering at the back of a cave filled with bones of animals she had eaten. As the story goes, they took her to the mainland, where she was identified as the missing girl. There is no record of what happened to her. See Fife, p. 150.

The other legend is of a Native American girl who was left behind when her tribe abandoned San Nicholas Island seventy miles off Santa Barbara in 1835. She is said to have lived alone for eighteen years until she was rescued. The novel by Scott O'Dell, *Island of the Blue Dolphins*, is based on the story. See Ellison, pp. 36–38, 77–89; O'Dell.

FIVE NIGHTMARES

The Dream: Some dreams come true because it is logical that they do so. For examples see Schwartz, *Telling Fortunes*, pp. 57–64. But this dream is a puzzle. The story is based on an experience reported by Augustus Hare in his autobiography, p. 302.

Sam's New Pet: I heard this story in Portland, Oregon, in 1987. It was one of many versions being told in that period. Folklorist Jan Brunvand entitled one of his collections of modern legends *The Mexican Pet*. In it he reprints a 1984 variant of this story from Newport Beach, California, as well as other versions. See pp. 21–23.

Folklorist Gary Alan Fine suggests that this legend reflects anger over Mexican workers who entered the United States illegally and competed for jobs held by Americans. The Mexicans are represented by a pet that turns out to be a rat. He cites a similar legend in France based on the arrival of workers from Africa and the Near East. See Fine, pp. 158–59.

Maybe You Will Remember: How the Story Ends.

What happened to Rosemary's mother?

When the hotel doctor saw Mrs. Gibbs, he knew at once that she was about to die. She had a form of the plague, a dread disease that killed quickly and caused frightening epidemics.

If the word got out that a woman had died of the plague in the heart of Paris, there would be panic. People in the hotel and elsewhere would rush to escape. The doctor knew what the hotel's owners expected. He was to keep the case a secret. Otherwise, they would lose lots of money.

To get Rosemary out of the way, the doctor sent her to the other side of Paris for some worthless medicine. As he expected, Mrs. Gibbs died soon after she left. Her body was smuggled out of the hotel to a cemetery, where it was buried. A team of workmen quickly repainted the room and replaced everything in it.

The desk clerks were ordered to tell Rosemary that she was in the wrong hotel. When she insisted on seeing her room, it had become a different place, and, of course, her mother had vanished. All those involved were warned that they would lose their jobs if they gave away the secret.

To avoid panic in the city, the police and the newspapers agreed to say nothing of the death. No police reports were filed; no news stories appeared. It was as if Rosemary's mother and her room had never existed.

In another version of the story, Rosemary and her mother had separate rooms. Mrs. Gibbs died during the night while Rosemary was asleep. Her body was removed. Then her room was repainted and refurnished. When Rosemary could not find her mother the next morning, she was told that her mother was not with her when she checked in.

After many months of searching, a friend, a relative, or the young woman herself finds someone who works in the hotel and, for a bribe, reveals what happened.

This legend was the basis of a movie, *So Long at the Fair*, that appeared in 1950. The story also inspired two novels, one published as early as 1913. But the story was old even then. The writer Alexander Woollcott discovered that it had been reported as a true story in England in 1911 in the *London Daily Mail* and in America in 1889 in the *Detroit Free Press*. It became known throughout America and Europe. See Woollcott, pp. 87–94; Briggs and Tongue, p. 98; Burnham, pp. 94–95.

The Red Spot: There are several versions of this legend in America and Great Britain. Spiders actually lay their eggs in cocoons or egg sacs that they spin from silk and leave in secluded places. Folklorist Brunvand suggests that stories like these grow from a common fear of having our bodies invaded by such creatures. See Brunvand, *The Mexican Pet*, pp. 76–77.

No, Thanks: This story is based loosely on one reported in *The New York Times*, March 2, 1983, p. C2.

WHAT IS GOING ON HERE?

The Trouble: When no cause could be found for the strange events in this story, many people wondered if a noisy, mischief-making ghost called a poltergeist was responsible. Stories of poltergeist hauntings have been common in our folklore for centuries. It was said that these poltergeists caused objects to fly and furniture to dance, pulled sheets and blankets from beds, made rapping and groaning sounds and other mischief.

At a ranch in Cisco, Texas, in 1881, something or someone threw rocks, opened locked doors without a key, squeezed raw eggs through the cracks in a ceiling, and mewed like a cat. Everything and everyone was checked, just as they were in "The Trouble." Some of what happened could have been caused by a prankster. But there were no explanations for much of it, except that a poltergeist had been at work. See Lawson and Porter.

Parapsychologists, such as the two in our story, are concerned with mental powers humans may have that are not yet understood. Psychokinesis (PK) and extrasensory perception (ESP) are examples of these powers.

"The Trouble" is based on news reports in *The New York Times*, *Life* magazine, and other publications. For stories of poltergeists and information on poltergeist research, see Carrington and Fodor, Creighton, Haynes, Hole, and Rogo.

WHOOOOOOOO?

Strangers: This brief tale is told in America and Britain. There are many settings for the story, including a turnip field and a museum.

The Hog: Ghosts are said to appear in many forms: as animals—in our story, a hog; as balls of fire and other lights; as living humans; and as specters. Some ghosts, of course, remain invisible, making their presence known only by their actions and sounds.

The story of the woman who returns as a hog is adapted and expanded from a Canadian ghost story told on Prince Edward Island. See Creighton, p. 206.

Is Something Wrong?: This story is expanded from a summary of an Afro-American ghost tale in Jones, "The Ghosts of New York," p. 240. It is related to a hoax tale about an encounter with a horrible monster. In that story, the monster is an escaped murderous lunatic. When he catches up with the man who is fleeing, he cries, "Tag, you rascal!" See Schwartz, *Tomfoolery,* p. 93, p. 116.

It's Him!: This is a version of the "Man from the Gallows" family of tales. It is adapted from two tellings. One is from the Cumberland Gap region of Kentucky; see Roberts, pp. 32–33. The other is in the University of Pennsylvania folklore archive. It was collected from Etta Kilgore in Wise, Virginia, in 1940, by Emory L. Hamilton. See the note to the story "Just Delicious."

T-H-U-P-P-P-P-P-P-P!: This story is an expansion of a

joke young children tell.

You May Be the Next...: This parody of the famous "Hearse Song" is from the folklore collection at the University of Massachusetts. It was contributed by Susan Young of Chelmsford, Massachusetts, in 1972. For a variant of the traditional song and its background, see Schwartz, *Scary Stories to Tell in the Dark*, p. 39, pp. 94–95.

Bibliography

BOOKS

Books that may be of particular interest to young people are marked with an asterisk (*).

Briggs, Katharine M. *A Dictionary of British Folktales.* 4 vols. Bloomington, Ind.: Indiana University Press, 1967.

————, and Ruth L. Tongue. *Folktales of England.* Chicago: University of Chicago Press, 1965.

*Brunvand, Jan H. *The Mexican Pet: More New Urban Legends and Some Old Favorites.* New York: W. W. Norton & Company, Inc., 1986.

*————. *The Vanishing Hitchhiker: American Urban Legends and Their Meanings.* New York: W. W. Norton & Company, Inc., 1981.

Burnham, Tom. *More Misinformation.* New York: Lippincott & Crowell, Publishers, 1980.

Carrington, Hereward, and Nandor Fodor. *Haunted People: Story of the Poltergeist Down the Centuries.* New York: New American Library, Inc., 1951.

Collison-Morley, Lacy. *Greek and Roman Ghost Stories.* Oxford: B. H. Blackwell, 1912.

*Creighton, Helen. *Bluenose Ghosts.* Toronto: Ryerson Press, 1957.

Curtin, Jeremiah. *Tales of the Fairies and the Ghost World: Irish Folktales from Southwest Munster.* London: David Nutt, 1895.

Ellison, William H., ed. *The Life and Adventures of George Nidever.* Berkeley, Cal.: University of California Press, 1937.

Hare, Augustus. *The Story of My Life*. London: George Allen & Unwin Ltd. An abridgment of Vols. 4, 5, and 6, George Allen, 1900.

Haynes, Renee. *The Hidden Springs: An Enquiry into Extra-Sensory Perception*, rev. ed. Boston: Little, Brown and Company, 1973.

Hole, Christina. *Haunted England: A Survey of English Ghost-Lore*. London: P. T. Batsford Ltd., 1940.

*Johnson, Clifton. *What They Say in New England and Other American Folklore*. Boston: Lee and Shepherd, 1896. Reprint edition, Carl A. Withers, ed. New York: Columbia University Press, 1963.

*Jones, Louis C. *Things That go Bump in the Night*. New York: Hill and Wang, 1959.

*Kipling, Rudyard. *The Jungle Book*. New York: Harper and Brothers, 1893.

Lüthi, Max. *Once Upon a Time: On the Nature of Fairy Tales*. Bloomington, Ind.: Indiana University Press, 1976.

*O'Dell, Scott. *Island of the Blue Dolphins*. Boston: Houghton Mifflin Company, 1960.

Randolph, Vance. *Ozark Superstitions*. New York: Columbia University Press, 1947. Reprint edition, *Ozark Magic and Superstitions*. New York: Dover Publications, Inc., 1964.

Roberts, Leonard. *Old Greasybeard: Tales from the Cumberland Gap*. Detroit: Folklore Associates, 1969. Reprint edition, Pikesville, Ky.: Pikesville College Press, 1980.

Rogo, D. Scott. *The Poltergeist Experience*. Harmondsworth, England: Penguin Books Ltd., 1979.

*Schwartz, Alvin. *More Scary Stories to Tell in the Dark*.

New York: J. B. Lippincott, 1984.

   *———. *Scary Stories to Tell in the Dark*. New York: J. B. Lippincott, 1981.

   *———. *Telling Fortunes: Love Magic, Dream Signs, and Other Ways to Tell the Future*. New York: J. B. Lippincott, 1987.

   *———. *Tomfoolery: Trickery and Foolery with Words*. Philadelphia: J. B. Lippincott Company, 1973.

   Shattuck, Roger. *The Forbidden Experiment: The Story of the Wild Boy of Aveyron*. New York: Farrar, Straus & Giroux, Inc., 1980.

   Shelley, Mary Wollstonecraft. *Frankenstein, or the Modern Prometheus*. Indianapolis: The Bobbs-Merrill Company, Inc., 1974.

   Thompson, Stith. *The Folktale*. Berkeley, Cal.: University of California Press, 1977.

   ———, ed. *Folk Tales and Legends*. The Frank C. Brown Collection of North Carolina Folklore, Vol. 1. Durham, N. C.: Duke University Press, 1952.

   Tongue, Ruth L. *Forgotten Folk-Tales of the English Counties*. London: Routledge & Kegan Paul Ltd., 1970.

   Van Paassen, Pierre. *Days of Our Years*. New York: Hillman-Curl, Inc., 1939.

   Widdowson, John. *If You Don't Be Good: Verbal Social Control In Newfoundland*. St. John's, Newfoundland: Memorial University of Newfoundland, 1977.

   Woollcott, Alexander. *While Rome Burns*. New York: The Viking Press, Inc., 1934.

   Yarborough, Willard, ed. *The Best Stories of Bert Vincent*. Knoxville, Tenn.: Brazos Press, 1968.

ARTICLES

Balfour, M. C. "Legends of the Lincolnshire Cars, Part 2." *Folklore* 2 (1891): 271–78.

Bertillion, L. D. "The Lobo Girl of Devil's River." *Straight Texas*. Publications of the Texas Folklore Society 13 (1937): 79–85.

Cox, John Harrington. "The Witch Bridle." *Southern Folklore Quarterly* 7 (1943): 203–9.

Fife, Austin E. "The Wild Girl of the Santa Barbara Channel Islands. *California Folklore Quarterly* 2 (1943): 149–50.

Fine, Gary Alan. "Mercantile Legends and the World Economy: Dangerous Imports from the Third World." *Western Folklore* 48 (1989): 153–62.

Graves, Robert. "Praise Me and I Will Whistle to You." *The New Republic*, Sept. 1, 1958, 10–15.

Jones, Louis C. "The Ghosts of New York: An Analytical Study." *Journal of American Folklore* 57 (1944): 237–54.

Lawson, O. G., and Kenneth W. Porter. "Texas Poltergeist, 1881." *Journal of American Folklore* 64 (1951): 371–82.

Lüthi, Max. "Parallel Themes in Folk Narrative and in Art Literature." *Journal of the Folklore Institute* 6 (1967): 3–16.

The New York Times. Articles in 1958 regarding incidents described in "The Trouble," a story in this book: issues of Feb. 3, 6, 7, 9, 20, 22, 24, 25, 27; Mar. 6, 26, 29.

———. "Stranger in the Night." Metropolitan Diary, Mar. 3, 1982, C2.

Parler, Mary Celestia. "The Wolf Boy." *Arkansas Folklore* 6 (1956): 4.

Wallace, Robert. "House of Flying Objects." *Life*, Mar. 17, 1958, 49–58. Regarding incidents in the story "The Trouble."

Ward, Donald. "The Return of the Dead Lover: Psychic Unity and Polygenesis Revisited." *Folklore on Two Continents: Essays in Honor of Linda Dégh*, 310–17. Eds.: Nikolai Burlakoff and Carl Lindahl. Bloomington, Ind.: Trickster Press, 1980.

Widdowson, John. "The Bogeyman: Some Preliminary Observations on Frightening Figures." *Folklore* 82 (1971): 90–115.

Acknowledgments

I thank the many boys and girls who asked for this third book of scary stories. I hope it pleases them. I also am grateful to the people who shared their stories with me and to the librarians and folklore archivists at the University of Maine at Orono, at the University of Pennsylvania, and at Princeton University for their help in my research. I thank Joseph Hickerson of the Library of Congress for identifying popular music based on the "vanishing hitchhiker" legend. And I am indebted as always to my wife and colleague Barbara Carmer Schwartz for her many contributions.

A.S.

ALVIN

work of more

young readers

and humor to tal

tions of scary sto

DARK, MORE SCARY S

STORIES 3, and two I

ROOM and GHOSTS!—ar

folklore collection.

STEPHEN GAMM

appeared in a number of bo

SCARY STORIES TO TELL IN THE DA

TELL IN THE DARK, and SCARY STOR

the Caldecott Medal for his drawi

MAN by Karen Ackerman. His art in

BEGIN by Olaf Baker earned him a C

Boston Globe–Horn Book Award, and a N

Illustrated Book citation. He also won a

for his art in THE RELATIVES CAME by Cynt

Gammell lives in St. Paul, Minnesota.

ALVIN SCHWARTZ is known for a body of work of more than two dozen books of folklore for young readers that explore everything from wordplay and humor to tales and legends of all kinds. His collections of scary stories—SCARY STORIES TO TELL IN THE DARK, MORE SCARY STORIES TO TELL IN THE DARK, SCARY STORIES 3, and two I Can Read Books, IN A DARK, DARK ROOM and GHOSTS!—are just one part of his matchless folklore collection.

STEPHEN GAMMELL's drawings have appeared in a number of books for children, including SCARY STORIES TO TELL IN THE DARK, MORE SCARY STORIES TO TELL IN THE DARK, and SCARY STORIES 3. He is the winner of the Caldecott Medal for his drawings in SONG AND DANCE MAN by Karen Ackerman. His art in WHERE THE BUFFALOES BEGIN by Olaf Baker earned him a Caldecott Honor, the *Boston Globe–Horn Book* Award, and a *New York Times* Best Illustrated Book citation. He also won a Caldecott Honor for his art in THE RELATIVES CAME by Cynthia Rylant. Mr. Gammell lives in St. Paul, Minnesota.

Acknowledgments

I thank the many boys and girls who asked for this third book of scary stories. I hope it pleases them. I also am grateful to the people who shared their stories with me and to the librarians and folklore archivists at the University of Maine at Orono, at the University of Pennsylvania, and at Princeton University for their help in my research. I thank Joseph Hickerson of the Library of Congress for identifying popular music based on the "vanishing hitchhiker" legend. And I am indebted as always to my wife and colleague Barbara Carmer Schwartz for her many contributions.

A.S.